This book belongs to

_____

Dedicated to our incredible village.

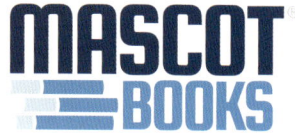

www.mascotbooks.com

Mama's Workout Buddy

©2018 Carina Parks. All Rights Reserved. No part of this publication may be reproduced, stored in a retrieval system or transmitted in any form by any means electronic, mechanical, or photocopying, recording or otherwise without the permission of the author.

Stroller Strides® is a registered trademark of Stoller Strides, LLC, dba FIT4MOM used with kind permission and under license with the company.

For more information, please contact:
Mascot Books
620 Herndon Parkway, Suite 320
Herndon, VA 20170
info@mascotbooks.com

Library of Congress Control Number: 2018908201

CPSIA Code: PRT0818A
ISBN-13: 978-1-64307-243-2

Printed in the United States

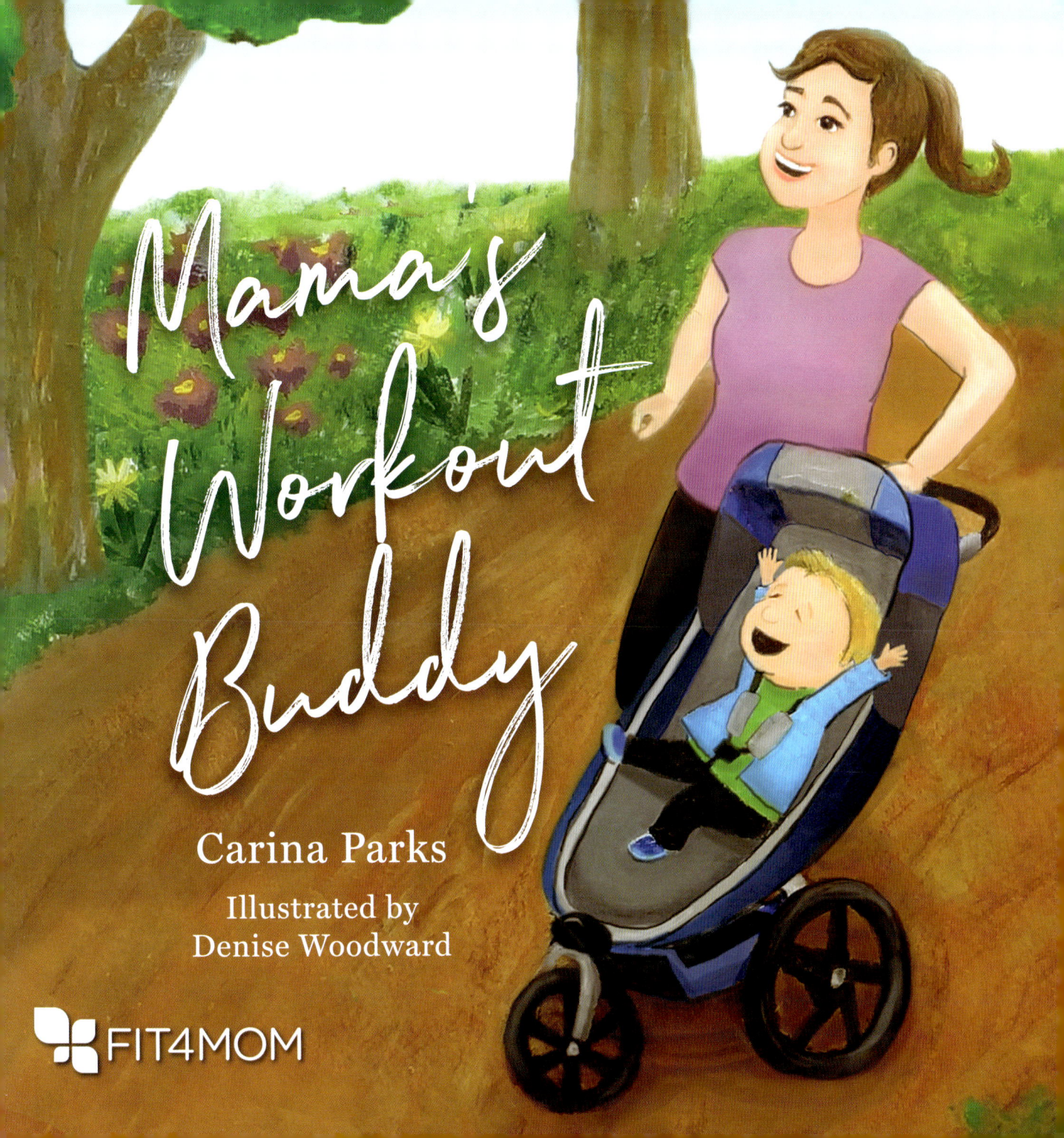

This is a story about witnessing Mama taking care of herself, so she can take the best care of me!

It's morning. Off to Stroller Strides we go!
Oh how Mommy and I need it so!
Mom has packed snacks for her and for me–
healthy ones, I'm sure they will be!

Maybe a yogurt, a crisp apple, or a pear;
When I see my friends, I love to share!

Today at the park is where we'll meet.
Mom unpacks the stroller and puts shoes on my feet.

I smell the fresh grass. I feel the warm breeze.
The bright yellow sun winks at me through the trees!

With big warm hugs, I greet all my friends.
On days we don't go, the day never ends!

The warm-up is fun! I listen out for my name.
On to Station One, where it's never the same!

What will the instructor have in store?
I can tell you this—it's never a bore!

Super-Moms to strengthen Mom's back.
Now give her one more jumping jack!

In a wall sit, she sings to me,
my favorite song—the ABCs!

Now she's running liners and I see a ball!
"Throw it to me!" Mom hears me call.

The instructor loves showing us pretty bubbles, almost as much as I love jumping in puddles!

Sadly, we're at the last Stroller Strides Station.
Squats and lunges are her destination.

Look at Mama working hard in the sun,
showing me that exercise can be so much fun!

The time has come for her to work her core for a while.
I listen for, "The most important stretch is a SMILE!"

That's my cue.
Out of the stroller,
I get.
Mama tells me to
watch my step.

Mommy has her
post-workout smile.
Now it's my turn to
play for a while.

My absolute favorite, it's playgroup time.
Stories, games, painting, or slime?!

Mama stands with her friends for a chat,
while I eat a snack on her yoga mat.

Tomorrow, after class,
we're off to the zoo.
I'm so excited!
My friends are coming
too!

With our village around us every step of the way,
Mama feels supported, and I can just play!

Stroller Strides Saves The Day!

Notes for Mama – What is Stroller Strides?

Stroller Strides® is a functional, total-body conditioning workout designed for moms with kids in tow. Each 60 minute workout is comprised of strength training, cardio, and core restoration, all while entertaining the little ones with songs, activities, and fun!

Each Stroller Strides instructor is skilled to meet you where you are mentally and physically. You'll leave class feeling connected, successful, and energized. No more Mama guilt! This class is all about self-care in a supportive and encouraging environment.

Brought to you by FIT4MOM®

About The Author And Illustrator

Carina Parks grew up in England and moved to California when she was pregnant with her daughter. Having no family close by, her love for FIT4MOM runs deep. She found Stroller Strides in 2013 when her daughter, Leah, was five months old, and she soon fell in love with her village of mamas whose support and friendship reached far beyond the workout. After the birth of her son, Ben, in 2015, Carina took over as Playgroup Captain, and in 2017, became an Instructor.

Carina currently resides in Sacramento with her husband and her favorite two workout buddies.

"Only work out on the days you want to feel great." —Lisa Druxman

Denise Woodward graduated from the illustration program at Brigham Young University in 2015. After graduation, she moved back to her hometown of Lexington, Kentucky, so her husband could attend medical school there. She is a children's book illustrator and a stay-at-home mom with one little boy at home, Collin, and another on the way.

Denise started FIT4MOM in September of 2017 to meet other moms, learn parenting tips, and feel great about working out to the ABC's. She's been hooked ever since. In her spare time, Denise enjoys hugging stuffed animals with her son and spending time with her little family.

@denisewoodward_art